This book belongs to:

Allison and Andrew

Printed in the U.S.A.

ISBN 0-7172-8286-4
Previously published as 0-681-40837-5

Jim Henson's
Muppet Babies
Baby Kermit's Opposites

by Bonnie Worth   illustrated by Kathy Spahr

GROLIER

UP

DOWN

SMILE

FROWN

WILD

TAME

It's the opposites game!

BOTTOM

TOP

GO

STOP

STAND

SIT

Get the hang of it?

DAY
NIGHT

LOOSE

TIGHT

FRONT

BACK

Get the knack?

CATCH

PITCH

POOR

RICH

WALK

RUN

Isn't this fun?

IN

OUT

WHISPER

SHOUT

GOOD

BAD

HAPPY

SAD

PUSH PULL

EMPTY FULL

BEGINNING

END
Play it with a friend.